Orville and Wilbur WRIGHT

The Brothers Who Invented the Airplane

SCIENTIFIC COLLABORATION

Orville and Wilbur WRIGHT

The Brothers Who Invented the Airplane

Gina Hagler

ROSEN PUBLISHING

Published in 2021 by The Rosen Publishing Group, Inc.
29 East 21st Street, New York, NY 10010

Library of Congress Cataloging-in-Publication Data

Names: Hagler, Gina, author.
Title: Orville and Wilbur Wright : the brothers who invented the airplane / Gina Hagler.
Description: New York : Rosen Publishing, 2021. | Series: Scientific collaboration | Audience: Grade 7-12. | Includes bibliographical references and index.
Identifiers: LCCN 2019013446 | ISBN 9781725342354 (library bound) | ISBN 9781725342347 (pbk.)
Subjects: LCSH: Wright, Orville, 1871-1948—Juvenile literature. | Wright, Wilbur, 1867-1912—Juvenile literature. | Aeronautics—United States—History—20th century—Juvenile literature. | Aeronautics—United States—Biography—Juvenile literature.
Classification: LCC TL540.W7 H245 2021 | DDC 629.130092/273 [B] —dc23
LC record available at https://lccn.loc.gov/2019013446

Printed in China

Photo Credits: Cover, pp. 3, 19 Library of Congress Prints and Photographs Division; p. 7 ullstein bild/Getty Images; p. 8 Kwirry/Shutterstock.com; pp. 11, 12, 25, 64–65 Donaldson Collection/Michael Ochs Archives/Getty Images; pp. 13, 52–53, 56–57 Universal History Archive/Universal Images Group/Getty Images; pp. 17, 60–61, 66 George Rinhart/Corbis Historical/Getty Images; pp. 18–19 Museum of Science and Industry, Chicago/Archive Photos/Getty Images; pp. 22–23 Albert Harlingue/Roger Viollet/Getty Images; pp. 26, 31, 50 Science & Society Picture Library/Getty Images; p. 28 Butterfly Hunter/Shutterstock.com; p. 33 Everett Historical/Shutterstock.com; pp. 36–37 Photo 12/Universal Images Group/Getty Images; p. 40 Hulton Archive/Getty Images; pp. 42–43 © AP Images; pp. 44–45 Fotosearch/Archive Photos/Getty Images; pp. 46–47 Hulton Archive/Archive Photos/Getty Images; Cover, back cover and interior pages design graphic LineByLine/Shutterstock.com.

CPSIA Compliance Information: Batch #BSR20. For further information contact Rosen Publishing, New York, New York at 1-800-237-9932.

CONTENTS

Introduction

It's difficult to imagine a time when people doubted that flight was possible. It's also difficult to imagine that people risked their lives to try anyway. The first unsuccessful attempts were made by those who thought that gluing feathers to their arms would make flight possible. These attempts were followed by unsuccessful tries by those who thought takeoff speed was the key. Additional failed attempts were made by those convinced that the flapping motion of the arms would make the difference.

Others used stories and drawings to imagine what flight might be like. One Greek myth tells of Icarus, a young man who used wings of wax and feathers. He flew too close to the sun, his wings melted, and he fell from the sky and drowned in the Mediterranean Sea. Leonardo da Vinci (1452–1519) drew a scene that shows a view of Earth that is said to only be possible when viewed from above. Designs for flying machines also occupied the minds of those intent on flight. Leonardo is just one of the people who drew flying machines that he thought might succeed.

In this image, Icarus is falling from the sky after daring to fly too close to the sun. Icarus's fall is often referred to when an attempt to do something bold and new is announced.

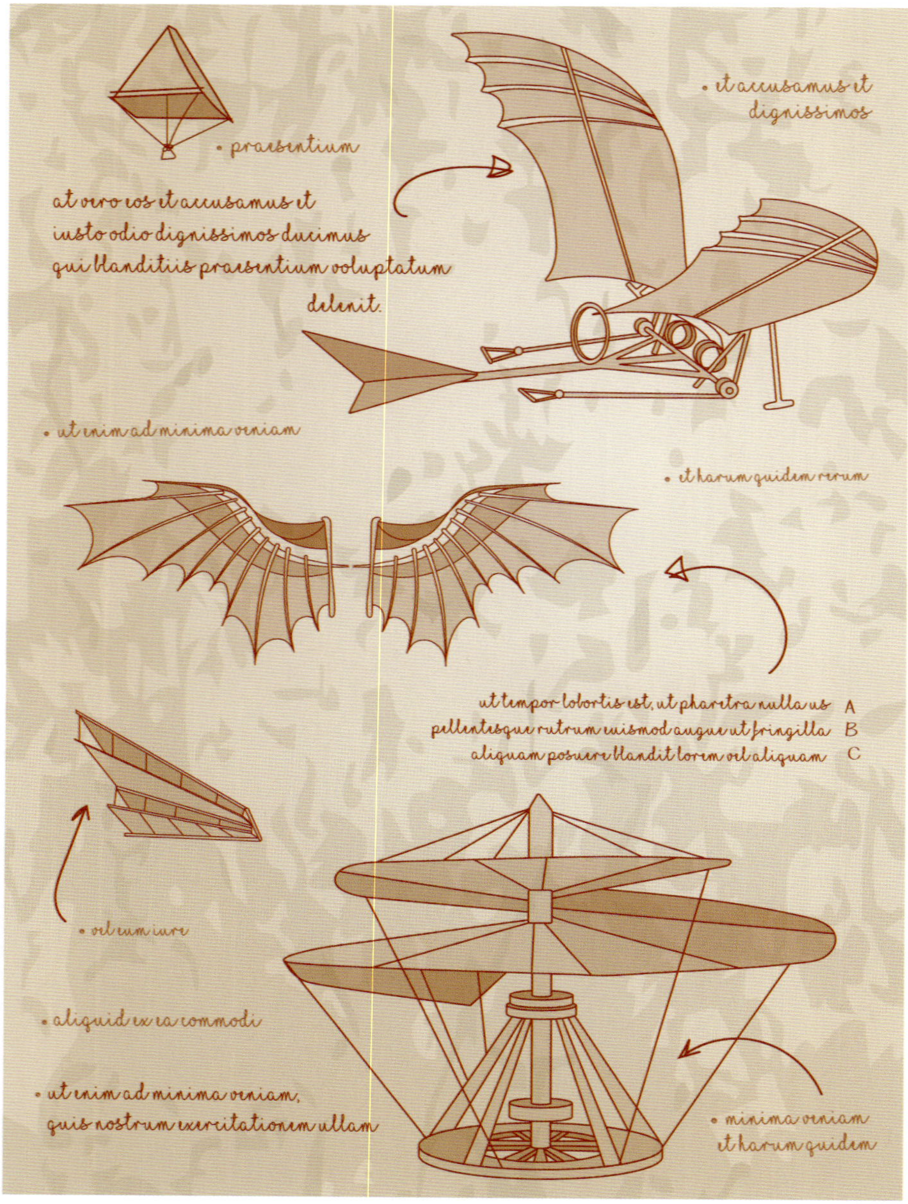

Leonardo da Vinci was one of the greatest thinkers of all time. His designs for parachutes, airplanes, and a helicopter were the result of his interest in flight.

It is now known that none of these dreamers were correct because none of them imagined the forces in play. Even after Sir George Cayley (1773–1857) named the aerodynamic forces of lift, thrust, gravity, and drag, the way they worked together wasn't obvious. If thrust didn't come from jumping off a building with feathers glued to the arms while flapping wildly and lift couldn't be attained by jumping off a hill while wearing canvas wings, then how did it work?

When Wilbur (1867–1912) and Orville (1871–1948) Wright were young men, the public was fascinated with the possibility of flight. People had seen toys that could fly for a short distance, had flown kites, and had observed birds taking off, hovering, and landing. They were also aware that things that were lighter than air could "float" in the sky in the form of gigantic hot-air balloons. Shouldn't it be possible to achieve controlled, heavier-than-air, powered flight with a machine? Orville and Wilbur wondered too.

The Wright brothers were first to solve the problem of flight. These brothers were ordinary men who worked together to achieve one of the greatest feats in aviation history. They worked as a team to design, test, and fly the first successful airplane—a powered, heavier-than-air object with a passenger aboard under control the entire time. Each brother working alone might have solved some of the problems that arose. By collaborating, they were able to successfully solve them all.

Wilbur and Orville Wright succeeded because they had a new approach and a successful collaboration. Their mutual respect made it possible to trade ideas back and forth. It allowed them to think outside the box to imagine new solutions. And, when things didn't go as expected, their working together gave them the confidence to discover why and to give it another try using what they'd learned. Their collaboration changed the world.

CHAPTER ONE

A Family on the Move

So much has been written about Wilbur and Orville Wright as young men that it's easy to forget they were once young boys. Before they grew up to work together to solve the problem of manned, heavier-than-air, powered flight, they played and explored, making friends and developing interests that would last their lifetimes. Just what were the Wright brothers like as children?

The Bishop's Boys

Wilbur and Orville were four years apart in age. They were the middle children, with two older brothers and one younger sister. Their father, Milton Wright (1828–1917), was an itinerant preacher who moved his family often as he went from state to state representing the Church of the United Brethren in Christ. The family moved from Indiana to Ohio to Iowa and back to Ohio as the family grew. Once Milton Wright was named a bishop in 1884, the family settled in Dayton, Ohio. It was here that Wilbur

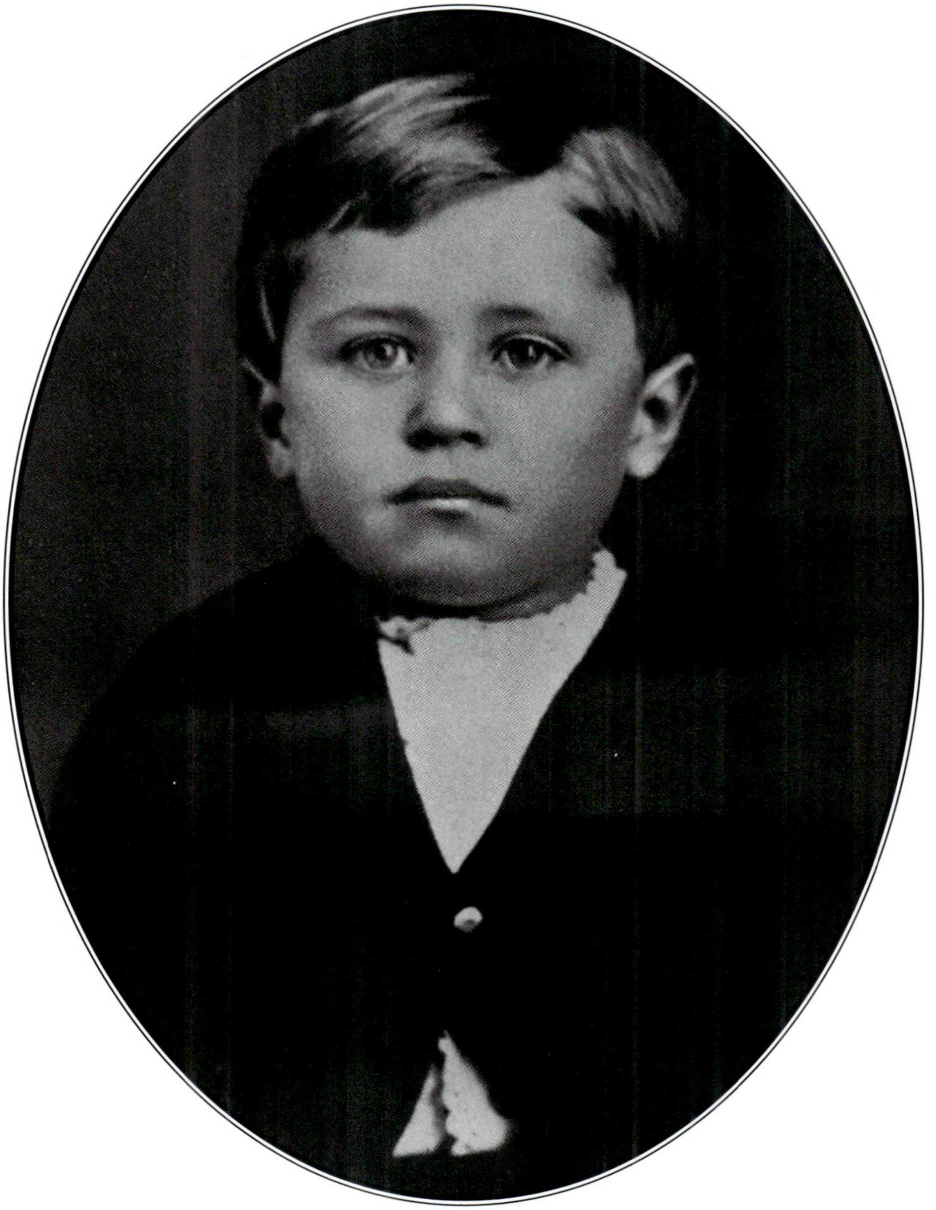

Orville Wright, six years old in this picture, was one of seven children. He and his brother Wilbur were especially close.

Wilbur Wright, nine years old in this picture, was the older of the famous Wright brothers. Although he was an excellent student, an accident during a hockey game kept him from attending college.

and Orville were known as the bishop's boys to the adults in town. To their friends, they were known as Wil and Orv.[1]

Moving often meant the brothers found themselves the new kids on a regular basis. This caused the boys to be close friends. Wilbur once commented that many of the toys they had belonged to both of them. Too young to be part of their older brothers' adventures, Wil and Orv made up games and inventions of their own. Wilbur was more studious than Orville. Orville was the shyer of the two. Throughout their lives, Wilbur would do the

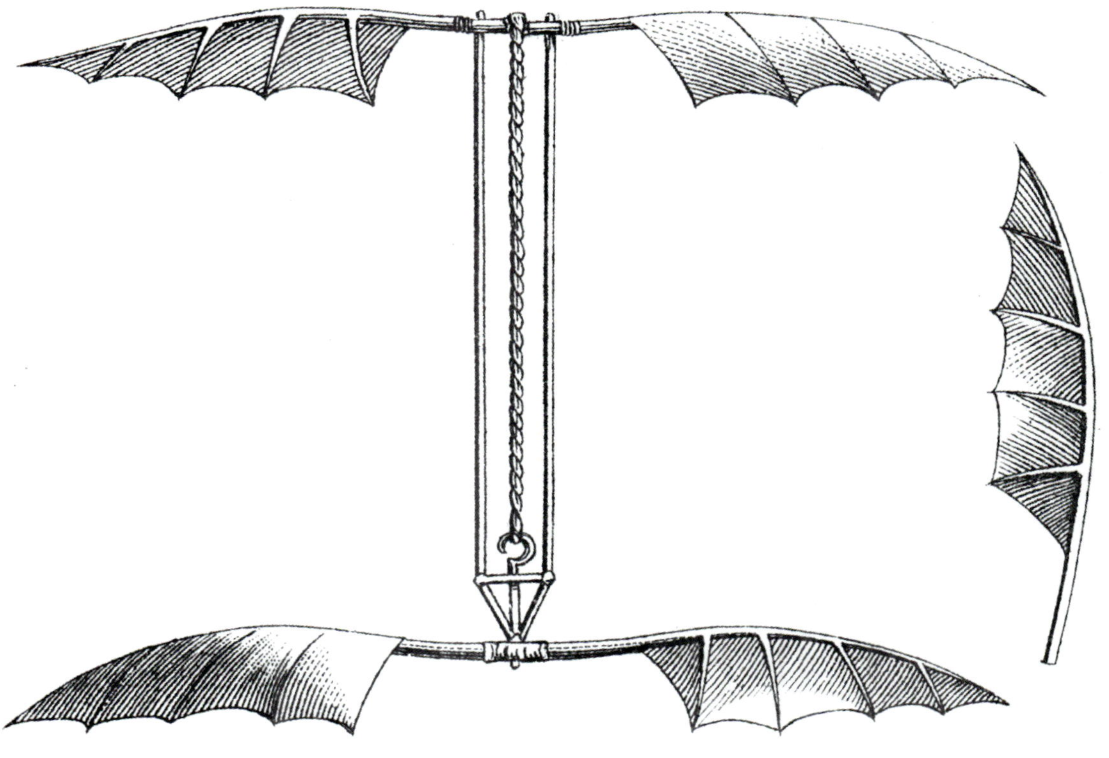

Alphonse Pénaud's planophore was an early helicopter. Wil and Orv were fascinated by this little flying craft.

The Pénaud Helicopter

Pénaud's helicopter, the planophore, was the first object to put the theories of George Cayley to use in a heavier-than-air machine that flew under its own power. It a) was heavier than air because it did not float, b) a machine because it was not a living thing, and c) flew under its own power because it was the unwinding of the rubber band that provided energy for flight. The "bat" also proved that a plane would level off once Cayley's forces of lift, drag, gravity, and thrust equaled out. The brothers observed that the toy flew straight up until it ran out of energy or hit the ceiling. Years later, Orville would name the toy and Alphonse Pénaud as among their earliest influences.

speaking for the both of them while Orville tinkered around with their inventions.

When Wil and Orv were young, there were no electric lights, radios, telephones, or televisions. There were no cars. There were no bicycles either. Railroads were fairly new to America. Since trains were the only things that could move faster than a team of horses, there seemed to be a set limit to the speed at which one could travel. Since the only things in the sky were birds and paper kites, it seemed impossible that anything other than a bird could fly very far under its own power or in a direction it chose.

All of that changed on the day in 1878 when Milton Wright returned from a trip with a new toy. It was a sort of helicopter, invented by French aeronautical inventor and engineer Alphonse Pénaud (1850–1880). Pénaud called the toy a Planophore: Wil and Orv called it "the bat." It used a rubber band for power. The first step was to twist the rubber band many times while holding the propeller still. When the propeller was released, it twirled. Pénaud's little helicopter astonished the brothers by flying up until it hit the ceiling.[2]

After several flights, the toy broke. Wil and Orv made many new versions of their own. Playing with the little helicopter gave them their first taste of flight. Their experience with the toy started a fascination that lasted their entire lives. It was a moment that they would remember. Orville even made a sketch of the toy fifty years later, in 1929.

Becoming Young Men

Throughout their teens, the Wright brothers worked at a variety of jobs. They invented and fixed things in a shop where they kept their equipment. Wilbur studied hard in high school. He planned to go to Yale, but those plans ended when he was hit in the face during a game of hockey. He had damage to his face and a concussion that resulted in a serious depression. He did not leave the house and studied on his own during the next three years. His mother was also dying during that time, and he took care of her.

While Wilbur was recovering from his depression and nursing his mother, Orville started a weekly newspaper called the *West Side News*. He was the editor and publisher until Wilbur joined him as a partner a few years later. With two of them to work on the paper, they extended their weekly coverage to nightly coverage and it became an evening newspaper.[3]

Their mother, Susan Wright (1831–1889), died a few months after Wilbur began the *West Side News*. When she died, Orville and Wilbur's younger sister, Katharine (1874–1929), became responsible for running the house. Katharine earned a college degree and became a teacher, and Orville and Wilbur went on to become famous aviators. Yet the three of them created a tight bond after their mother's death. That bond lasted for the rest of their lives.[4]

In 1890, Orville agreed to print the *Tatler*, Dayton's first weekly African American newspaper, for friend Paul Laurence Dunbar, who would go on to become a celebrated poet, novelist, and playwright. Orville continued in the printing and newspaper business for many more years. The brothers even started a weekly magazine called *Snap Shots* in 1894. By 1896, they were done with the newspaper business. The bicycle had captured their attention and was taking more and more of their time.[5]

The Bicycle Shop

It wasn't until the 1890s that the bicycle became popular in the United States. Both Wilbur and Orville bought their first bikes in 1892. They loved to ride and race. Soon after buying bicycles of their own, they opened the Wright Cycle Exchange. It was their first bicycle shop. They sold bikes from the many companies of the time. They did repairs, taught people to ride, rented bikes, and sold parts and accessories. The bicycle shop changed locations six times before Wilbur and Orville settled on a shop that was the right size in the right place.

One factor that influenced the location was based on a business decision that helped the bicycle store to thrive. Wilbur and Orville decided to establish their shop right near where the League of American Wheelmen held their twelfth annual meeting in 1896. Wilbur and Orville were members of the organization and knew that thousands of cyclists would visit the city to race and tour. Their new location made it certain that, while on the tour, the visiting cyclists would pass right by the Wright Cycle Exchange.

The bicycle shop would be the main source of income for the brothers for many years. Running the shop used both their

It was in this building in Dayton that the Wright brothers did their experimentation with their wind tunnel. This work helped them solve the "problem of flight" and fly successfully at Kitty Hawk, North Carolina, in 1903.

skill sets to the best advantage. Wilbur was comfortable speaking with the customers. Orville was comfortable fixing the bikes and experimenting with new ideas. He had also invented a calculator that could both multiply and add.

Aeronautical Fever

With a sure source of income during the cycling season, Wilbur and Orville were free to dream of flight during the winter. Shortly after the shop opened, they attended the aeronautical exhibit at the World's Columbian Exposition in Chicago in May 1893. Their fascination with the idea of manned, heavier-than-air, powered flight had endured from their childhood experience with the bat. Meanwhile, news of German aeronautical pioneer Otto Lilienthal (1848–1896) had reached the United States. The news included photographs of Lilienthal dressed in his flying gear and moving through the sky. Both Wilbur and Orville were fascinated by the work done with gliders by Lilienthal.[6]

The World's Columbian Exposition in 1893 brought entrepreneurs and visitors from around the world. It was one of several expositions that showcased the latest inventions.

The Wrights weren't the only ones watching Lilienthal's adventures. Lilienthal caught the attention of the world and proved that man could successfully glide through the sky with some small measure of control. If Lilienthal could manage this, perhaps working from what he'd accomplished would put powered flight within reach. Now in their twenties, the Wright brothers had worked together to run a newspaper and print papers for others. With their bicycle store doing well, they were ready to turn their talents and attention to the question of flight.

CHAPTER TWO

It's in the Wings

The "problem of flight" had existed since humans first tried to understand how it was that birds could fly while people could not. It made no sense to human observers that these little feathered creatures could flap their wings and rise from the ground and into the air, but they could not lift themselves at all by flapping. They could only lift themselves from the ground for seconds at a time by jumping.

Long before George Cayley identified the forces at work in flight in 1799 and etched them on a silver disc, Leonardo da Vinci had sketched various flying machines in the late 1400s. Both of these men had ideas that would influence others, but it was Cayley's glider that proved a heavier-than-air object could stay in the air. By 1888, Pénaud was able to put these principles to work in the toy the Wright brothers called the bat. The next step was for someone to put these principles in action with a powered, manned flight.

Death of the "Flying Man"

In the early days of aviation, there were easily more failures than successes. One spectacular success was Lilienthal. He was known as the "flying man" because he wore wings and a harness with a lower bar for steering. He flew gliders (today known as hang gliders) by taking off from a hill and steering with his body weight as he flew through the air.

In an era before mass media, it often took a long time for people on one continent to learn about what happened on another. This was not the case with Lilienthal. In the 1890s, photographs and stories appeared in publications in the United States and Europe. Lilienthal was known as "the father of flight" because he was the first to make his way through the air. It's true that he did not have a source of power. It's also true that he did not take off from the ground. What he did do was prove that it was possible for a heavier-than-air, manned object to fly distances of up to 820 feet (250 meters) when the conditions were right.[1]

Otto Lilienthal was known as the "flying man." He wore wings and launched himself from a hilltop. His wing design and flying technique was much like the hang gliders of today.

Lilienthal had his last flight on August 9, 1896. For some reason, the glider headed straight for the ground. Lilienthal wasn't able to steer the glider at that angle. All he could do was crash from a height of about 49 feet (15 meters). He broke a vertebra and was hurried away in a wagon. A famous surgeon operated on him the next day, but it was not enough. Lilienthal died about thirty-six hours after the crash.[2]

For the many would-be aviators who learned of the crash and Lilienthal's death, this was devastating news. For the Wright brothers, who had been following the news of Lilienthal's flights, it served as a warning of what could happen to them. It also caused them to make decisions in their attempts at flight that put their personal safety above other considerations.

The Wright Cycle

Shortly before Lilienthal's fatal crash, Wilbur and Orville decided to manufacture their own bicycles. The first cycles were known as the Van Cleve and the St. Clair. Their bicycles came with some choices and many new features that the brothers invented. For the first years, cycle sales were very good, and Wilbur and Orville earned three to six times as much as most workers. They were also able to save several thousand dollars. This money would go to their flying experiments.[3]

By 1898, there was too much competition in the cycling market. Large manufacturers came in and sold their products for a lower price. Ultimately, this would drive many shops and manufacturers, such as the one owned by the Wright brothers, out of business. Until that happened in the early 1900s, the brothers would use whatever income they made from their shop to pay for their work in aeronautics. They also had their equipment and tools available for their work on solving the question of flight.[4]

Wilbur and Orville Wright were "tinkerers." They used the materials on hand to create the tools they needed to get the job done. Here, Wilbur is busy at their workbench.

The Four Forces of Flight

George Cayley, also known as "the Father of Aeronautics," was an English engineer and aviator who named the four forces of flight in 1799:

- **Lift is the force of the wind beneath the wing. As it rushes over the top of a wing with a broad front edge and a narrow back edge, the air going over the larger height and the air moving directly below the fixed wing create an upward force.**
- **Thrust is the power that moves the airplane forward.**
- **Drag is the friction caused by the "skin" of the airplane.**
- **Gravity is the force that pulls everything to Earth.**

Sir George Cayley understood and was the first to name the four forces of fixed-wing flight. His work in aerodynamics provided the background for the work done by early aviators.

When all of the forces are balanced, an airplane will stay in flight at a constant speed in a constant direction.

A Cautious Approach

Wilbur and Orville were anxious to create a flying machine, but they were not ready to take unnecessary risks. Otto Lilienthal's death was a constant reminder that what they were doing could be not only dangerous but deadly. To be sure they had the best chance of success without injury, the brothers started slowly, testing their concept at each step to be sure it worked.

The Twisted Wing

Up until 1899, all experiments at flight had used the weight of the person flying to control the movement of the plane. In the case of Lilienthal, this meant that when he was unable to shift his weight to change the direction of the glider, the glider crashed. Wilbur and Orville, who had watched as hawks and buzzards flew overhead, had observed that these flyers did not shift their body weight to control their direction. They seemed to be doing something with their wings. Whatever it was, it also made it possible for the birds to stay aloft.

It's certain the brothers spent many hours discussing the possibilities before the day in the summer of 1899 when Wilbur discovered that moving the opposite corners of a long narrow box together caused the wings to twist, or warp. This twisting motion, he realized, would make it possible to control the direction of flight by causing a kite with a top and bottom wing to roll. The rolling action would move one half of the wing up while the other half of the wing tilted down. This motion would cause the glider to turn. It would also increase the lift.[5]

After making several sketches and inventing a way to control the wings as well as the body of the kite, the brothers built what is known as the 1899 experimental kite.[6] The kite flew beautifully. The wind lifted it into the air where it stayed and flew steadily.

The strings that controlled the wings worked as planned, and the glider could roll as intended.

Studying Flight

Wilbur and Orville now threw themselves into the work of building a plane that would carry a man under its own power. The kites and gliders they'd build from now on would be models to test their theories. At each step, they would check that their ideas worked before moving on.

The Wright brothers watched birds hovering above them. From their actions, they could see how lift worked to keep the bird aloft. They also watched the way birds used their wings while in the air.

The study of birds in flight occupied a great deal of their time. They observed the flying behavior of birds in all kinds of weather. They noted what the wings did, what the tail did, and how it all worked together to keep the birds under control and in the air. The brothers understood that lift had to be generated while in the air if a bird or plane were to stay in the air.

They might be able to supply power and work with the drag and the force of gravity. Lift was something that had to be generated by the craft while it was in flight. Flight was not possible without balancing the four forces of flight.

As the Wright brothers prepared to focus on flight, they consulted with others who were involved in experiments in aeronautics. They were eager to learn what was known and to use that knowledge in their own work. They knew about Lilienthal's work with aerodynamics, in addition to his work with the glider. It was not unusual at this time for early aviators to share their work with others interested in flight. Many times, these findings were reported as papers at meetings of engineers or in volumes that were distributed by the Smithsonian in Washington, DC.

CHAPTER THREE

Two Failed Gliders

As the nineteenth century drew to a close, an increasing number of inventors stepped up to try their solutions for the problem of flight. The Wrights must have felt pressure to begin their work before the first successful flight was undertaken by someone else. When the US government stepped up to fund Samuel Pierpont Langley's attempts at flight with his Aerodrome, it was clear the time for a successful airplane flight was now.[1] The Wright brothers had no choice but to begin their work immediately, at their personal expense.

On May 30, 1899, Wilbur contacted the Smithsonian Institution to request any papers they had related to flight. "I am an enthusiast but not a crank," he wrote. "I wish to avail myself of all that is already known and then if possible add my mite to help on the future worker who will attain that success." Included in the papers available was the 1894 *Progress in Flying Machines* by Octave Chanute. This paper, along with his work with multi- and bi-wing gliders, was well known to those in aviation.[2]

Samuel Pierpont Langley was certain his Aerodrome would be the first heavier-than-air object to fly successfully under its own power. His attempts to launch from a houseboat on the Potomac River were unsuccessful.

The Chanute Letter of 1900

In addition to reading the work of Chanute and other early aviators, the Wrights began a correspondence with Chanute in 1900. Chanute was easily among the most prominent authorities on flight in the world. He was also in communication with most of the aeronautical pioneers. It was through him that the Wrights could obtain reliable information on the latest happenings. He also offered advice. His position at the center of the network of aviation pioneers made it possible for him to see a larger picture that was not available to each individual or team working alone.

Wilbur's 1900 letter to Chanute told Chanute about the brothers' belief that flight was possible to man. In the letter, he told Chanute that he was prepared to spend a few months pursuing his interest in flight. He mentioned his studies of birds and the plans he and his brother had to make their first attempts as safe as possible for themselves. With this letter, Wilbur made it clear that he and Orville were serious about solving the problem of flight. He also made it clear that they had done a great deal of study and put a great deal of thought into how to go about it.[3]

Wilbur also mentioned Lilienthal in the letter. He, and presumably Orville, were convinced that Lilienthal crashed for two reasons that they could avoid. One reason was that Lilienthal had invested hundreds of hours of time and effort into the problem of flight to spend only five hours of actual flying time. Wilbur was certain it would take more time than that to be able to control a craft during flight. The second reason he named was that Lilienthal's glider was flawed from the start by the inability to control it by any means except shifting the weight of the pilot. This made it nearly impossible to control anything more than the tilt of the plane from side to side. Wilbur wrote that he and Orville had studied birds and decided that the ability to shift course was due to special properties of birds' wings and the way birds used their wings.[4]

From the start, it was clear in their correspondence with Chanute that the Wright brothers were cautious men. They wanted to be the first to fly, but they also wanted to survive the

Octave Chanute designed a series of gliders during the summer of 1896. The success of his gliders gained Chanute recognition among the early aviators. His glider served as an inspiration to the Wrights.

attempt. The fate of Lilienthal was a permanent and alarming reminder of what could happen before a potential aviator could log enough flying experience. The correspondence with Chanute described a fairly impractical scheme to allow the brothers to fly without injury, but ultimately the Wright brothers would have to do their best and take their chances.

Kitty Hawk and the First Gliders

Wilbur and Orville were confident that their approach to flight would be successful. They would use Lilienthal's calculations in conjunction with their theory of wings to build a glider that could not fail to fly and remain aloft. They would then use this success to practice flying before moving on to powered flight. They chose Kitty Hawk, North Carolina, to test their first gliders because of the constant winds and sandy beaches. The winds would allow them frequent opportunities to test, tinker, and test again. The sandy beaches would provide a more forgiving landing than would an open field.

1900 Glider

The 1900 glider was the first to be tested at Kitty Hawk. It was an entirely new aeronautical design. It was the first to have a wing that could be controlled in all four directions. Not only could the nose be directed up or down, but the wings could use the wing warping the brothers invented to roll the glider to the left or right. This elevator, the part of the plane that makes it go up or down, gave the Wrights far more control over their glider, which was really a large kite, than Lilienthal or Chanute had ever had with their inventions.

To design the glider, Wilbur and Orville used all the knowledge they had gained by reading, watching birds, and speaking to Chanute. They also used what they knew about increasing speed in bicycle racing and shaped the glider so that the wind would flow off the tail. They planned to put one brother on board and have that brother practice flying with the glider. To do this, they would need as much lift as possible to get the glider into the air and to stay in the air for the time needed to practice controlling the glider.

The brothers were able to control the glider from the ground by using cables to move the controls. The glider worked very well except that it did not fly as high as they had calculated. It also could only carry a person on board when it was very windy. The few times Wilbur was able to catch a ride, he was happy to see that it all worked with him at the controls in the air. Clearly, their ideas and approach worked. The only problem was that the glider was not generating enough lift.[5]

Diagnosing the Problem

The Wrights hadn't picked the size of their glider wings at random. They'd used the lift coefficients used by Otto Lilienthal in his own work, along with another number known as the Smeaton coefficient. When the 1900 glider didn't perform as expected, Wilbur and Orville went back through all their calculations and designed the 1901 glider with larger wings. When this glider also failed to fly as calculated, the Wrights reviewed every measurement and angle. Lilienthal's lift coefficients showed again and again that the gliders should be doing better, but the Wrights could not be sure unless they could test both the lift and the drag of the airfoil, or shape of the wing, for themselves. This was essential to their work, but it had never been done before.

1901 Glider

Back in Dayton, the Wrights worked on increasing the lift of their glider. If making it lighter or using the shape to make it more aerodynamically sound wouldn't work, they would find

The Wright brothers were cautious aviators. They planned and tested at each step of the way. One of their first tests was on their 1901 glider. They compared what they expected to what occurred, then used those results in their future attempts.

something else that would. They tried several things and finally decided the wing needed a larger wing area.

The 1901 glider had nearly twice as much wing area. The idea behind this was that it gave the wind a larger surface to push against and flow around. As a result, greater lift should be produced. The brothers had also made other changes to the design, all to increase lift.

When they tested it at Kitty Hawk, the results were truly disappointing. Not only did the large wings make the glider harder to control, they also failed to increase the amount of lift. This left Wilbur and Orville with a larger, clunkier glider than the first one. Thoroughly discouraged as they left for Dayton, Wilbur told Orville that man might one day fly, but it wouldn't be in their lifetimes or even in a thousand years.[6]

While they worked to find and fix the problem in their calculations, Wilbur and Orville also found that the bike business wasn't as strong as it had been. Competition had increased. Cyclists could now buy bikes from many more manufacturers. Their income was not as steady as it had been. This didn't keep them from continuing in their quest for flight, however.

CHAPTER FOUR

The Wind Tunnel

After both their gliders failed, Wilbur and Orville could easily have given up. They'd thought about flight and studied birds and papers for years. They'd calculated and theorized and put all of their money into solving this one grand problem. Now, their cycling shop was not doing well, and the results from their work with the gliders made no sense. Instead of a sleek flying machine that could carry a human (and a power source) aloft, they had produced two gliders that solved the problems of control but could not gain sufficient lift.

The Need for a Wind Tunnel

Wilbur and Orville made a living by manufacturing bicycles of their own design. They understood, through experience, what it took to get a machine moving and what it took to keep it moving. They had seen for themselves that some designs helped a rider to go faster than others. They'd learned through schooling, observation, and reading the work of others. They were dedicated to their work on their flying machine, but they were not known for their sophisticated work areas or tools.

When the Wrights needed a piece of equipment they didn't have, they improvised and rigged up something made with what they had on hand. Their attention to detail, combined with their skill in building things, often resulted in just what was needed to do the job. With the gliders, the brothers had put tremendous time and effort into their calculations, only to find that their numbers were off. When they decided to do aerodynamic tests of their own, they knew they would need to build a wind tunnel.

The First Wind Tunnel

Wind tunnels were nothing new. Frank H. Wenham (1824–1908) built the first one in Great Britain in 1871 with funds from the Aeronautical Society of Great Britain. The wind tunnel had a body that was a long box with an opening on both sides. On one side, there was a fan that blew air into the box. At the other end was an opening for the stream of air to exit the box without causing turbulence inside the box. Each airfoil being tested was mounted in the box with instruments that could measure the air as it flew over, under, and around the airfoil.[1]

The measurements taken were then used to compare the performance of the different shapes. Which wing shape would perform the best? Would it be a completely flat wing? Would it be a wing that was thicker at the back than at the front? Would it be the opposite, with the thicker edge at the front with a tapering to the back? Any question about the shape of the wing could be tested in the wind tunnel.

The shape of the wind tunnel was important. The way the air entered the tunnel was vital. The flow of air needed to be steady. It needed to reach the airfoils in a stream that was like the stream of air that would pass over the wing. Gusts of wind might be tested eventually, but the first test must identify the best shape to begin with.

The Wright Wind Tunnel

The Wrights actually built two wind tunnels. The first was to test the concept. They built this with material they had around the shop. They recorded their first measurements on scraps of wallpaper they put in the bottom of the tunnel. Once they could see that their findings differed from Lilienthal's and that there was

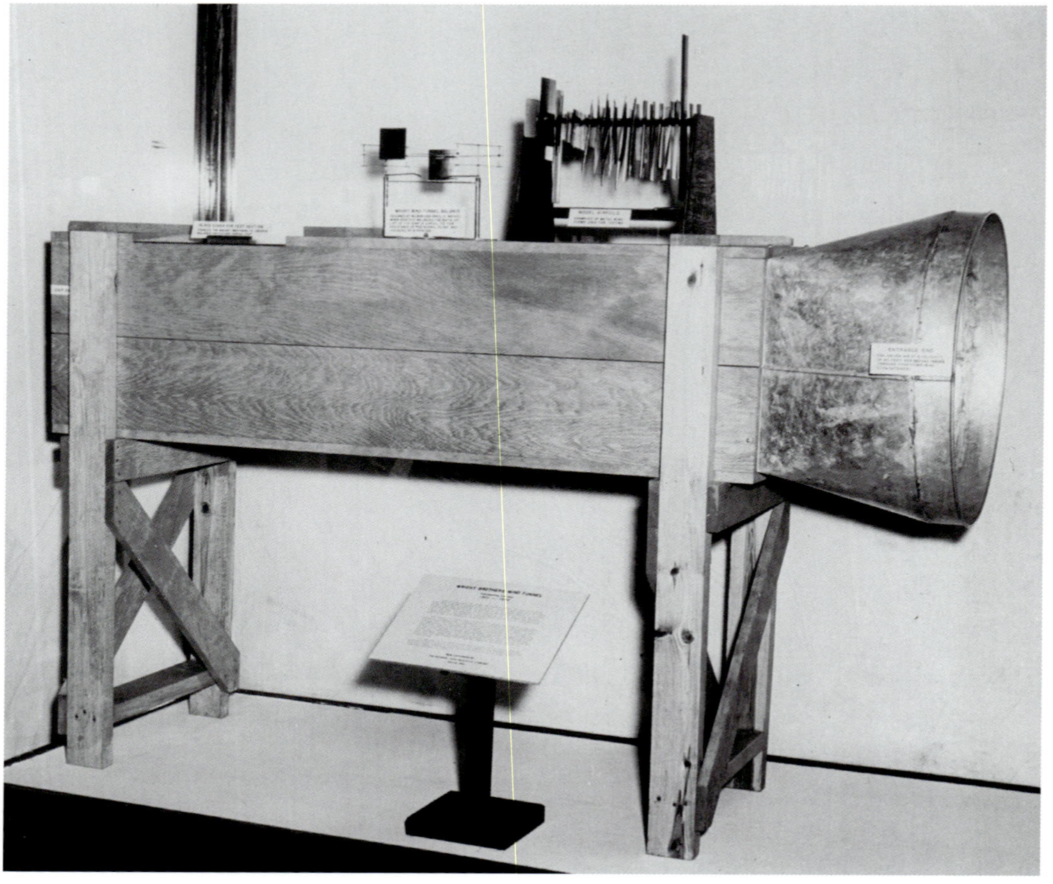

The Wright wind tunnel was essential to the Wright brothers' success. It was with this machine that they were able to test wing shapes and test more than one force of flight at a time.

tremendous value in performing these wind tunnel tests, they put their time and effort into building a larger wind tunnel.[2]

The second wind tunnel was larger. After some trial and error, they were able to have the air flow through the tunnel for reliable results. The only problem was that no one could move around on the second floor of the building where the wind tunnel sat without disturbing the airflow and results. To get around this, they put a glass window in the top of the wind tunnel so they could observe what was happening inside. With this wind tunnel, the Wrights tested more than forty different airfoils in a two-month period. Chanute offered to fund them so that they could conduct additional research during the bicycle season, but the brothers declined. They had to be open for business if they wished to keep their customers.[3]

Specialized Equipment to Measure Lift and Drag

After their unsuccessful attempts to fly their gliders, the Wrights needed a set of accurate figures to use in their calculations before trying again. The best tests and results would need to take both the lift and the drag into account, but there was no way to test both of these at the same time—if at all. By developing one balance to test lift and another to test drag, the brothers could not only calculate more meaningful measurements but also calculate their own lift coefficient. The calculation of this coefficient proved vital to their work. It not only indicated that Smeaton's coefficient was incorrect, but it gave them the accurate coefficient they needed to achieve success.

The First Aeronautical Engineers

The measurements the Wrights took during that two-month period in 1901 revolutionized the field of aerodynamics. Rather than put a shape on a long string and swing it overhead in a circle while taking measurements to see how the shape performed (a method that caused too much turbulence to be very accurate) or walking away from their work when the results did not meet their expectations, the Wrights took a scientific approach to uncovering what had gone wrong. They also used a scientific approach to determine what might work better.

A wind tunnel is a sophisticated piece of equipment before the instruments and work even begin. Attaching a piece of metal to a stationary pole inside the wind tunnel might provide useful information. Designing specialized equipment that could move the airfoil in a variety of ways as the air flowed past it would provide information that was even more useful. With that in mind, the Wrights invented two balances, one for lift and one for drag, to give them more meaningful readings. They would put the balance inside the wind tunnel to hold the airfoil and position it precisely during testing. This piece of equipment did not exist until the brothers made the first one. True to their ability to build something never before seen out of something used every day, Orville built the balancing vane out of old hacksaw blades and bicycle spokes.[4]

The instruments they designed gave them the ability to control the position of the airfoils as the wind rushed past. Because they recognized that air flowing past an object would give the same results as an object moving through air, they were able to visualize the different positions an airfoil might

Orville examines the balances that were used in the wind tunnels. It was these balances that made it possible for the brothers to use their observations in tests that perfected the shape and performance of their airfoils.

Orville watches Wilbur take readings before a flight in 1908. The Wright brothers were the first aeronautical engineers. They took measurements and used them to help them ensure successful flights under varying conditions.

have as it moved through the air and mimic those movements inside the wind tunnel.

The result of their two months of work was the most technologically sophisticated work of science in the field of aerodynamics to date. When the Wrights said that a wing should be thicker at the front edge than the back edge, they had the data to prove it. When they spoke about the angle of camber, they were not making a guess. Their work changed the way work in aerodynamics would be done far into the future.

Their wind tunnel and balances provided the Wrights with the information they needed to design a wing that was aerodynamically sound, one that would generate the greatest amount of lift given the drag, gravity, and thrust involved. It also made it possible for the Wrights to accurately predict the performance of the wing before that wing was built. This, in turn, made it possible for them to design an airplane that would meet the requirements for heavier-than-air, powered, manned flight.

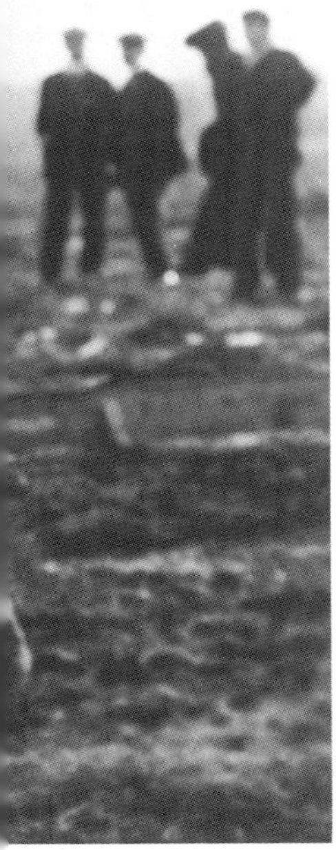

The Wrights might have come up with a wing design through trial and error alone, but that is unlikely. There were many others working in exactly that way, including others working with different concepts and figures of their own. The genius of the Wrights—and the thing that made them the first aeronautical engineers—was their ability to take what had been done before, test their findings through the lens of engineering with equipment of their own design, and complete all of this with their own money in the time they had between bicycle seasons.

CHAPTER FIVE

Success!

The Wright brothers had put their lifelong interest in aviation into action back in 1899. They'd cautiously taken all they knew and put it to work in the experimental kite. They had followed that success with additional study and careful calculation of what should work. They'd based first their 1900 glider and then their 1901 glider on their study and experience. When those gliders had failed to perform as expected, they'd conducted their own methodical wind tunnel tests on different airfoils to find a wing shape that would generate the lift needed for successful flight. Confident that they now had what they needed to succeed, Wilbur and Orville prepared for the flight of their newest glider.

The 1902 Glider

The 1902 glider was the first fully controllable airplane. It had a rudder; control in the directions of up, down, and forward motion; two wingspans, one above the body of the airplane and one below; and wing warping. It was a large machine, with

Orville Wright flies a biplane glider at Kitty Hawk, North Carolina, in 1902. This successful flight proved that a man could be carried aloft over a distance. The next step was to add power and systems for steering and to control the altitude of the plane.

wings measuring 32 feet (9.8 m) from tip to tip. The surface area of the wings had been calculated for maximum lift.[1]

For the first time, it was Orville at the controls. Before that, Wilbur had been the one on board during the glides.[2] In much the same way Wilbur had crashed earlier gliders, Orville crashed this one. That didn't stop them from continuing their collaboration. They rebuilt the glider and, while they were at it, made a few changes to the control system so that it would work more in the way they had in mind.[3]

The successes the brothers had could not help but attract attention, no matter how careful they were to keep their progress to themselves. While the 1902 tests were under way, Orville and Wilbur were visited by their older brother and several aeronautical inventors, including Chanute. One of them had even helped design the 1896 biplane glider that had first given

Location, Location, Location

Lilienthal had his man-made hill. Langley had his catapult on the Potomac. The Wright brothers had Kitty Hawk. Each selected a site for their work that they thought would give them the strongest possible advantage. For Lilienthal, the existence of a specific place with a known height provided the flying man with the perfect platform for leaping into the air. For Langley, his catapult on the Potomac provided him with a clear line of flight and a landing on water that would not destroy his craft. For the Wright brothers, the fact that the US Weather Bureau listed Kitty Hawk as a spot with prevailing winds—coupled with soft sand and a lack of people nearby—made it the perfect location for their work.

the Wrights the inspiration for their own gliders. Clearly, it wasn't just the brothers who thought they were on the verge of success.[4]

The Wright Flyer

When Chanute arrived in the fall of 1902, he brought news of Langley's work for the government. Despite Langley's extensive education and experience, he still had not succeeded. The army had backed him and was counting on him to develop a plane for their use. His results had been dismal, and now the army had given him one more year to succeed with his Aerodrome. If he did not, they would withdraw their support for his work.[5]

Wilbur and Orville's methodical approach and caution had seen them through from the experimental kite to the series of gliders. They had spent years and their own money perfecting their design. They had met their goal of spending enough time in the air to feel experienced with flying a glider, and as a result of their time in the air, they had proven they were able to control a glider. Now, it was time for them to move on to powered flight. If they could achieve this before Langley, it would be the achievement of a lifetime. It was a lot of pressure, but they likely were excited at the possibility.

The Gasoline Engine

Once the Wrights felt ready for powered flight, they set to learning all they could about engines. Many of the other would-be powered-flight aviators of the time used steam engines, but Wil and Orv decided a gasoline engine would better suit their purposes. There were no gasoline engines manufactured at that time that could meet their needs, so the brothers designed, built, and tested an engine of their own design. A mechanic they employed produced many of the parts in the brothers' bicycle shop.[6] Once again, the brothers collaborated and invented the

The Wright brothers were the first to use an onboard engine to generate power for their aircraft while in flight. The engine needed to be lightweight and reliable. The motor made it possible for their plane to travel longer distances.

right tool for the job—this time with the care and precision demanded for their goal of powered flight.

The Wright engine generated thrust by using matching propellers at the rear of the aircraft. These propellers—based on the work the brothers had done in their wind tunnel—counter-rotated. They did not spin in the same direction at the same time in order to provide a balanced force to push the engine forward. To keep the engine from overheating, it was cooled by water stored in a radiator. They included a flywheel to prevent vibrations and a magneto to generate electricity that was used for the system that started the engine.[7]

There were four cylinders that acted as the combustion chambers. They worked to ignite a fuel/air mixture the same way that simple combustion chambers work today. The other parts of the engine were also like the modern simple engines. They included a fuel line, timing chain, air intake, carburetor, and lubrication system. Though it was simple, this engine had about twice the power of a gas-powered lawn mower.[8]

The First Successful Flight

Wilbur was usually at the controls when the brothers tested an airplane. For this special flight, they tossed a coin. Wilbur won, and it was he who was on board for the flight on December 14. He rose too fast. The engine stalled and the airplane dove nose first into the sand. They couldn't try again until repairs were made.[9]

On December 17, Orville was the pilot. The wind that day was blowing nearly as fast as their predicted speed of 30 to 35 miles (48 to 56 kilometers) per hour. That would make things difficult but not impossible. Orville controlled the ascent of the plane, rising more slowly than Wilbur had a few days before. The wind wasn't the only factor that made this flight tricky;

this new airplane was larger and heavier than any they had flown before.[10]

There is an iconic photo that shows the moment Orville took off in the Wright Flyer at 10:30 a.m. The plane has run down the metal rail they used to guide it during takeoff and is

Orville Wright rises into the air on the first successful powered, heavier-than-air flight on December 17, 1903. The flight lasted twelve seconds and flew 120 feet (37 meters).

barely off the ground. Wilbur has run alongside and now stands beside the right wing. What will happen next is unknown in that moment. Orville could just as easily have crashed as flown. The plane could just as easily have been destroyed as returned to the ground in good condition.

It is known now that Orville managed to keep the plane in the air for 120 feet (37 m). It was a bumpy ride as the wind blew, and he struggled to keep the four forces of flight in balance. The Wright Flyer reached an airspeed of 34 miles per hour (55 kmh). It landed safely. Their airplane was a success.

Wilbur and Orville took turns flying the airplane three more times. The more experience they had, the farther they flew. On the last flight of the day, with Wilbur at the controls for the second time, the airplane flew 852 feet (260 m) in 59 seconds.[11]

The Wright Flyer served its purpose. Wilbur and Orville took to the sky in a heavier-than-air, powered, controlled airplane. The wind took a toll, though, and after the fourth flight of the day the plane got caught by a gust that caused it to roll over. The damage was too much to easily repair. They'd have to build a new flyer for the next season.

That afternoon, they sent their father a telegram to tell them what they'd accomplished.[12]

News Spreads Fast

Wilbur and Orville had known they were about to make history. They'd dressed in coats and ties for the flights on December 17. They'd sent a brief telegram to their father to share the news with him, but they hadn't counted on the news getting out immediately with the telegram.

The *Virginian-Pilot* published the news on their front page the next day. The headline read: "Flying Machine Soars 3 Miles in Teeth of High Wind Over Sand Hills and Waves at Kitty Hawk on Carolina Coast."[13] The newsman who wrote the story hadn't actually been at Kitty Hawk. He got the information in bits and pieces from a variety of sources. Much of the information was incorrect.

On January 5, 1904, Wil and Orv made their official statement to the Associated Press. They provided the details of the flights and said that after they were done, they'd returned home "knowing the age of the flying machine had come at last."[14]

CHAPTER SIX

Beyond Kitty Hawk

Now that the brothers had flown successfully, they were ready to patent their flying machine as the first step in creating a business around their invention. They realized there were some adjustments that needed to be made before the plane would be fully practical and able to perform well under a variety of conditions, but they were up for the challenge. They also recognized that with powered flight, they would not need the persistent winds of Kitty Hawk. They decided to do the rest of their flying at Huffman Prairie, near Dayton, Ohio.[1]

A Practical Flying Machine

As the brothers spent more time in the air and worked to perfect their flying machine, they were faced with the reality that the control system still needed more work. Much of that work involved the elevator, which controlled the ascent and descent of the plane. Improvements to the elevator became a serious focus for them after a crash of the Flyer III in July 1905. In that crash, Orville smashed to the ground at more than 30 miles per hour (48 kmh). As the plane bounced along the ground, Orville

was thrown over the wing. Clearly, the elevator needed some work. They also paid some additional attention to the rudder.[2]

They decided that moving the elevator closer to the wings would increase the amount of control the pilot had. They also decided to put it a bit farther away from the center of the plane. They increased the length of the rudder. They also gave the propellers a new "bent-end" to keep the propellers from flattening. This was an essential change since the propellers lost thrust when they flattened.[3]

By August, they were ready to fly again. When the Flyer III climbed into the air, it was immediately obvious that this airplane was superior to those that had come before. Not only was it easier to control, but the landings were incident free. The airplane remained in the air until the gas tank ran dry—more than eighteen minutes—on September 26. By October 3, Orville flew for more than thirty minutes.

As was the case with the successful glider flights and the first successful powered flight, word spread and a crowd gathered. On October 5, with Wilbur at the controls, the Flyer III stayed in the air for thirty-nine minutes. It traveled

By 1905, Orville Wright piloted this version of an airplane. It was one of many successful flights in the years after the first at Kitty Hawk, North Carolina.

more than 24 miles (38.6 km). Once again, it landed only when it ran out of gas. The total time for that one flight was longer than the combined time in the air in 1903 and 1904. The 1905 Flyer III was the first airplane that could perform well enough to be considered a practical plane.[4]

Their successes attracted so much attention that the Wrights stopped their tests until they were awarded their patent and could find a buyer for their aircraft.

Patents and Contracts

It's typical that when a new invention is created, the inventor files a patent to protect that invention. The patent makes it illegal for any other individual, group, or company to use that invention for profit without the permission of the inventor. For the Wright brothers, a patent on the control system was of vital importance if they wanted to have the exclusive right to that system. Without the patent, anyone could profit from the years of work the brothers had invested in their flying machine.

There was a lot at stake, since the company that held the patent of the control system would be the company that was most likely to sell the airplane commercially and to the military. The military market for the airplane was very large and included other countries in addition to the United States. Every nation wanted to be able to protect its borders by having an air force that could keep invaders out.

In 1906, a patent was awarded by the US Patent Office to the Wright brothers for their airplane control system. With this patent in hand, they were now able to seek contracts for their airplanes. The first contracts were from French investors and the US Army. But there was one catch. To get the contract with the US Army, the Wright brothers had to show that their planes could perform in the ways the US Army needed. This included the manufacture and success of a two-passenger airplane.[5]

US Army

The Wright brothers had a contract with the US Army in mind from the time the 1905 Flyer achieved its impressive results. They knew that their plane would be of use to the military. They also knew that they were the only ones who could deliver such an aircraft. The first negotiations with the Army didn't get very far because the brothers hadn't been awarded a patent. They didn't want to share the details of their control system without a patent. The Army wasn't interested in purchasing something that might work; they needed to know that it did work, and also how it worked.

When the patent was awarded, the brothers were quick to approach the Army with the details they required. The Army also wanted proof. This proof was the proof that required the demonstration that led to a fatal crash in 1908. The demonstrations that led to that crash also led to a strong interest by the Army, especially once the problem was fixed and additional demonstrations were held. Governments in Europe were also interested as a result of the tests required by the US Army.

The Army couldn't just award the contract to the Wright brothers. They needed to open the contract up to bidding so that anyone with an airplane that could do the job could have a chance. Since they were certain the Wright Flyer would and could do what they needed, they wrote the specifications in a way that made the Wright brothers the obvious choice.[6]

The brothers couldn't be in America and Europe at the same time, so in 1908, Wil and Orv split up. Wilbur traveled through Europe making demonstrations. Orville performed the demonstrations in the United States. All went well until

The First Fatal Crash

Wilbur and Orville had crashed often, but they'd always been able to walk away. That wasn't the case on September 17, 1908. On that day, Orville was piloting the Wright Model A aircraft in a demonstration at Fort Myer, Virginia. His passenger was Lieutenant Thomas Selfridge (1882–1908). Selfridge was flying with Orville as part of a series of tests for the airplane in front of an audience of two thousand. Orville had flown many successful tests before Selfridge joined him, but when the airplane was 150 feet (46 m) in the air they experienced trouble. The plane would not respond to controls. The plane crashed and Selfridge died instantly. Orville was severely injured with a broken leg, several broken ribs, and assorted bumps and bruises.[7,8]

The Wright Model A airplane was the first Wright airplane to be part of a fatal crash. Despite the brothers' caution and attention to detail, the Model A Orville flew at the demonstration did not respond to controls. It crashed with Orville and Thomas Selfridge on board.

September 1908, when a two-passenger airplane piloted by Orville crashed during the demonstration. The cause of the crash was quickly corrected, but the first fatal crash was a sad day for the new aviation industry.[9]

Commercial Success

The Wright brothers knew that companies would be interested in their airplanes as a way to move their goods from place to place. It would be decades until the business model for a commercial airline to move passengers would be developed, but that didn't keep companies around the world from wanting to know more about these aircraft and see them in action.

Events were held in Europe. The Salon de l'Aéronautique was held in December 1908 in Paris. It would become an annual show and grow into the Paris Air Show that is still held. Today it is the world's largest show of its kind.[10]

Wherever they visited, the brothers were recognized and respected for their talent and the fact that they were the first to fly.

Conclusion

The Wright brothers would remain active in aviation for the rest of their lives. In 1910, they opened a flight school in Montgomery, Alabama, for civilian pilots. They also released the Wright Model B. This would become their most successful commercial airplane. In 1911, the Wright Company delivered the US Navy's first airplane, but ultimately it was the Curtiss Company that would provide the bulk of the seaplanes purchased by the Navy. After so many years of struggle, Wil and Orv had achieved success in financial terms as well as technical accomplishments.

Wilbur Wright died of typhoid in 1912. Orville went on to receive additional recognition for their work. He also fought Curtiss in a patent war when Curtiss rebuilt the 1903 Langley Aerodrome with improvements and claimed it may have flown before the Wright Flyer. The 1906 patent became the first of the airplane patents, but in 1914, the Smithsonian published a report that stated that Langley's Aerodrome was the first aircraft capable of flight. They made this claim based on Curtiss's rebuilt and improved version of the Aerodrome.[1]

Once Wilbur and Orville proved that flight was possible, others were eager to build airplanes of their own. The Wright brothers' Model B airplane was adapted for use in a race in 1910.

Beginning with the sale of his part of the Wright Company in 1915 and choosing not to renew his lease on the bicycle shop in 1916, Orville consulted on matters of aviation until his death from a heart attack in 1948. He was also honored with numerous awards and designations, one of which was Honorary Pilot's License No. 1, issued by Congressional decree.

Five years before Orville's death, the Smithsonian designated the Wright brothers as the first to fly a controlled, sustained, powered flight. Today the original 1903 Flyer is on display at the National Air and Space Museum in Washington, DC. In the same building, there is the first plane to break the sound barrier, a lunar module, and a piece of a moon rock.

By collaborating and thinking outside the box, these amazing brothers truly changed the world. They laid the foundation for aeronautical and astronautical innovations for years to come. Testing airfoils in a wind tunnel was just one step in the use of model testing that

Wilbur and Orville were brothers, friends, and collaborators. It was their mutual respect, shared vision, and hard work that made powered, manned, heavier-than-air flight a reality. Their collaboration changed the world.

continues to this day in the design of craft that will travel through a fluid such as water or air.

The quiet resolve of the Wright brothers has served as an inspiration to the generations of aeronautical and astronautical engineers who have followed. Their invention—the heavier-than-air, powered, manned aircraft—is the basis of the entire commercial airline industry. Today, this worldwide web of connecting flights makes it possible for goods and people to travel the globe.

Those who followed the Wrights went on to use their work as the basis of their own in inventing ever more powerful and sophisticated flying machines. Some of them, such as the space shuttle, would make their way beyond Earth's atmosphere and safely back. Wilbur and Orville Wright remain well known to anyone who studies the history of aviation. Their collaboration is a model to others who dream big and work diligently to succeed.

CHRONOLOGY

- **1867** Wilbur Wright is born in Indiana on April 16.
- **1871** Orville Wright is born in Ohio on August 19.
- **1878** Milton Wright brings home a Pénaud helicopter for the brothers.
- **1886** Wilbur is seriously injured in a hockey game.
- **1892** The brothers open the Wright Cycle Exchange.
- **1893** Wilbur and Orville attend the World's Columbian Exposition in May.
- **1894** Octave Chanute's *Progress in Flying Machines* is published.
- **1896** German aviation pioneer Otto Lilienthal dies on August 10.
- **1898** The US government underwrites Samuel Pierpont Langley's experiments in flight after the start of the Spanish-American War.
- **1899** Wilbur request materials on flight from the Smithsonian Institution on May 30; the Wrights test their experimental kite in July.
- **1900** The brothers begin their correspondence with Octave Chanute; the 1900 Wright glider is tested at Kitty Hawk, North Carolina, in October.
- **1901** The 1901 Wright glider is tested at Kitty Hawk in July; Wilbur presents Some Aeronautical Experiments to the Western Society of Engineers in Chicago, Illinois, in September at Chanute's invitation; the Wright wind tunnel is used to test airfoils that winter.
- **1902** The redesigned glider is tested at Kitty Hawk in the fall; the Wright Cycle Exchange closes.
- **1903** The Wright Flyer flies under power and with a man on board on December 17 at Kitty Hawk.
- **1904** The Wright Flyer II is tested at Huffman Prairie near Dayton, Ohio.

- **1905** The Wright Flyer III flies and crashes on June 23, leading to important changes in design.
- **1906** The Wright brothers receive US Patent 821393 for a "Flying Machine" on May 22.
- **1908** Wilbur and Orville sign a contract with a French company and the US Army.
- **1912** Wilbur dies on May 30.
- **1948** Orville dies on January 30.

CHAPTER NOTES

Chapter One A Family on the Move

1. "An Unusual Childhood," Wright Brothers Aeroplane Company, http://www.wright-brothers.org/History_Wing/Wright_Story/Unusual_Childhood/Unusual_Childhood_Intro.htm (accessed April 23, 2019).
2. History.com Editors, "Early Life," History, https://www.history.com/topics/inventions/wright-brothers (accessed April 23, 2019).
3. "Wilbur Wright," Smithsonian National Air and Space Museum, https://airandspace.si.edu/exhibitions/wright-brothers/online/who/1859/wilbur.cfm (accessed April 23, 2019).
4. "Wilbur Wright."
5. "Wright Bros., Job Printers," Smithsonian National Air and Space Museum, https://airandspace.si.edu/exhibitions/wright-brothers/online/who/1889/printers.cfm (accessed April 23, 2019).
6. "Otto Lilienthal," To Fly Is Everything, Mississippi State University, http://invention.psychology.msstate.edu/i/Lilienthal/Lilienthal.html (accessed April 23, 2019).

Chapter Two It's in the Wings

1. Carroll Gray, "Otto Lilienthal: 1848-1896," Flying Machines, http://www.flyingmachines.org/lilthl.html (accessed April 23, 2019).
2. Gray.
3. "Wright Bicycles," Wright Brothers Aeroplane Company, http://www.wright-brothers.org/Information_Desk/Just_the_Facts/Bicycles/Wright_Bicycles.htm (accessed April 23, 1019).
4. "Wright Bicycles."
5. Will Livingston, "The Wright Flyer's Warping Wings," Bio-aerial Locomotion 2011, October 18, 2011, http://blogs.bu.edu/biolocomotion/2011/10/18/the-wright-brothers-flyer.
6. Carroll Gray, "The First Five Flights," The Wright Brothers, http://www.thewrightbrothers.org/fivefirstflights.html (accessed April 23, 2019).

Chapter Three Two Failed Gliders

1. William E. Baxter, "Samuel P. Langley: Aviation Pioneer," Smithsonian Libraries, http://www.sil.si.edu/ondisplay/langley/intro.htm (accessed April 23, 2019).
2. "The Road to the First Flight," National Park Service, updated April 14, 2015, https://www.nps.gov/wrbr/learn/historyculture/theroadtothefirstflight.htm.
3. "Wilbur and Orville Wright Papers at the Library of Congress," Library of Congress, https://www.loc.gov/collections/wilbur-and-orville-wright-papers/articles-and-essays/the-belief-that-flight-is-possible-to-man (accessed April 23, 2019).
4. "Wilbur and Orville Wright Papers at the Library of Congress."
5. "The Road to the First Flight."
6. "The Road to the First Flight."

Chapter Four The Wind Tunnel

1. "Whirling Arms and the First Wind Tunnels," National Aeronautics and Space Administration, updated June 12, 2014, https://www.grc.nasa.gov/www/k-12/WindTunnel/history.html.
2. "The Wright Wind Tunnel," Smithsonian National Air and Space Museum, https://airandspace.si.edu/exhibitions/wright-brothers/online/fly/1901/wind.cfm (accessed April 23, 2019).
3. "The Wright Wind Tunnel."
4. "The Wright Wind Tunnel."

Chapter Five Success!

1. "The 1902 Glider," Smithsonian National Air and Space Museum, https://airandspace.si.edu/exhibitions/wright-brothers/online/fly/1902/glider.cfm (accessed April 23, 2019).
2. "Wagging Its Tail," Wright Brothers Aeroplane Company, http://www.wright-brothers.org/History_Wing/Wright_Story/Inventing_the_Airplane/Wagging_Its_Tail/Wagging_Its_Tail.htm (accessed April 23, 2019).
3. "Wagging Its Tail."
4. "Wagging Its Tail."

5. "Wagging Its Tail."
6. "Wright 1903 Aircraft Engine," National Aeronautics and Space Administration, updated November 20, 2018, https://wright.nasa.gov/airplane/eng03.html.
7. "Wright 1903 Aircraft Engine."
8. "Wright 1903 Aircraft Engine."
9. "1903-The First Flight," National Park Service, updated April 14, 2015, https://www.nps.gov/wrbr/learn/historyculture/thefirstflight.htm.
10. "1903-The First Flight."
11. "1903-The First Flight."
12. "Telegram from Orville Wright in Kitty Hawk, North Carolina, to His Father Announcing Four Successful Flights, 1903 December 17," World Digital Library, September 22, 2014, https://www.wdl.org/en/item/11372/.
13. David Shedden, "Today in Media History: Front-page News About the Wright Brothers 1903 Flight," Poynter, December 17, 2014, https://www.poynter.org/reporting-editing/2014/today-in-media-history-front-page-news-about-the-wright-brothers-1903-flight.
14. "Inventing a Flying Machine," Smithsonian National Air and Space Museum, https://airandspace.si.edu/exhibitions/wright-brothers/online/fly/1904/index.cfm (accessed April 23, 2019).

Chapter Six Beyond Kitty Hawk

1. "Huffman Prairie Flying Field," National Park Service, updated February 5, 2018, https://www.nps.gov/daav/learn/historyculture/huffman-prairie-flying-field.htm.
2. "A Practical Flying Machine," Wright Brothers Aeroplane Company, http://www.wright-brothers.org/History_Wing/Wright_Story/Inventing_the_Airplane/Practical_Flying_Machine/Practical_Flying_Machine.htm (accessed April 23, 2019).
3. "A Practical Flying Machine."
4. "A Practical Flying Machine."

5. "Wright Timeline 1900 to 1909," Wright Brothers Aeroplane Company, http://www.wright-brothers.org/History_Wing/Wright_Story/Wright_Timeline/Wright_Timeline_1900_1909.htm (accessed April 23, 2019).
6. "Wright Timeline 1900 to 1909."
7. "Selfridge, Thomas Etholen," National Aviation Hall of Fame, https://www.nationalaviation.org/our-enshrinees/selfridge-thomas-etholen (accessed April 23, 2019).
8. Jennifer Rosenberg, "The First Fatal Airplane Crash," ThoughtCo., updated April 29, 2018, https://www.thoughtco.com/the-first-fatal-airplane-crash-1779178.
9. "Military Use of the Airplane," National Air and Space Museum, https://airandspace.si.edu/exhibitions/wright-brothers/online/age/1910/military.cfm (accessed April 23, 2019).
10. "Commercial Aviation," Smithsonian National Air and Space Museum, https://airandspace.si.edu/exhibitions/wright-brothers/online/age/1910/commercial.cfm (accessed April 23, 2019).

Conclusion

1. "Wright Timeline 1910 to 1919," Wright Brothers Aeroplane Company, http://www.wright-brothers.org/History_Wing/Wright_Story/Wright_Timeline/Wright_Timeline_1910_1919.htm (accessed April 23, 2019).

GLOSSARY

aeronautical Having to do with the field that designs, builds, and flies aircraft.

airfoil The shape of an airplane wing.

astronautical Having to do with the field that designs, builds, and flies spacecraft.

camber The arched shape of an airplane wing.

drag The force of friction on an object in motion.

exclusive Can be used by only one person or group of people.

gravity The attraction of Earth's mass on an object.

iconic Widely known and easily recognized.

improvise To make, invent, or arrange from what is convenient or on hand.

itinerant Traveling from place to place.

lift The force produced when a fluid passes over and below a cambered surface.

magneto An electric generator.

mass media The various ways that media such as the news or entertainment reaches a large audience at one time.

rigged up Put together for use on a temporary basis.

rudder A part used for steering an object through a fluid such as water or air.

sophisticated Complex.

thrust The forward motion of an object.

tinker To try different things to make something work.

turbulence Unsteady air, water, or other fluid.

FURTHER READING

BOOKS

Crouch, Tom D. *The Bishop's Boys: A Life of Wilbur and Orville Wright*. New York, NY: W.W. Norton & Company, 2003.

Ford, Lily. *Taking to the Air: An Illustrated History of Flight*. London, UK: The British Library, 2018.

Grant, R. G. *Flight: The Complete History of Aviation*. New York, NY: DK, 2017.

Hampton, Dan. *The Flight: Charles Lindbergh's Daring and Immortal 1927 Transatlantic Crossing*. New York, NY: William Morrow Paperback, 2018.

McCullough, David. *The Wright Brothers*. New York, NY: Simon & Schuster, 2016.

Tise, Larry E. *Hidden Images of the Wright Brothers at Kitty Hawk*. Stroud, UK: The History Press, 2019.

WEBSITES

Library of Congress: Wilbur and Orville Wright Papers
www.loc.gov/collections/wilbur-and-orville-wright-papers/about-this-collection
Check out an online selection of the Wright brothers' original papers.

Smithsonian National Air and Space Museum: The Wright Brothers
airandspace.si.edu/exhibitions/wright-brothers/online/
Learn more about the Wright brothers, their work, and the beginning of the aerial age.

Wright Brothers Aeroplane Company
www.wright-brothers.org
Explore a virtual museum of all things relating to the Wright brothers.

INDEX